D1504210

RUDOLPH THE RED-NOSED REINDEER

RUDOLPH
THE RED-NOSED REINDEER
by Robert L. May

Illustrated by Michael Emberley

ISBN: 1-55709-294-X

FIRST EDITION

Thank you for purchasing an Applewood Book.
Applewood reprints America's lively classics—books from the past that are still of interest to modern readers. For a free copy of our current catalog, please write to Applewood Books, 18 North Road, Bedford, MA 01730.

10 9 8 7 6 5 4 3 2 1

Library of Congress Cataloging-in-Publication Data
May, Robert Lewis 1905-1976
    Rudolph the Red-Nosed Reindeer / by Robert L. May; illustrated by Michael Emberley. — 1st ed.
        p.   cm.
    Summary: Although the other reindeer laugh at him because of his bright red nose, Rudolph proves his worth when he is chosen to lead Santa Claus's sleigh on a foggy night.
        ISBN 1-55709-294-X
    [1. Reindeer—Fiction.   2. Christmas—Fiction.   3. Stories in rhyme.]
    I. Emberley, Michael, ill.   II. Title.
PZ8.3.M4525Rs   1994
[E]—dc20   94-20997
                                                            CIP
                                                            AC

Twas the day before Christmas, and all through the hills
The reindeer were playing . . . enjoying the spills
Of skating and coasting, and climbing the willows . . .
And hop-scotch and leap-frog (protected by pillows!)

While every so often they'd stop to call names
At one little deer not allowed in their games:—
"Ha ha! Look at Rudolph! His nose is a sight!"
"It's red as a beet!" "Twice as big!" "Twice as bright!"

While Rudolph just wept. What else could he do?
He knew that the things they were saying were true!
Where most reindeer's noses are brownish and tiny,
Poor Rudolph's was red, very large, and quite shiny.
In daylight it dazzled. (The picture shows that!)
At night time it glowed, like the eyes of a cat.
And putting dirt on it just made it look muddy.
(Oh boy was he mad when they nicknamed him "Ruddy!")

Although he was lonesome, he always was good . . .
Obeying his parents, as good reindeer should!

That's why, on this day, Rudolph almost felt playful:—
He hoped that from Santa (soon driving his sleighful
Of presents and candy and dollies and toys
For good little animals, good girls and boys)
He's get just as much . . . and this is what pleased him . . .
As the happier, handsomer reindeer who teased him.
So as night and a fog, hid the world like a hood,
He went to bed hopeful; he knew he'd been good!

While way, way up North,
    on this same foggy night,
Old Santa was packing
    his sleigh for its flight.

"This fog," he complained, "Will be hard to get through!"
He shook his round head. (And his tummy shook, too!)
"Without any stars or a moon as our compass,
This extra-dark night is quite likely to swamp us.
To keep from collisions, we'll have to fly slow.
To keep our direction, we'll have to fly low.
We'll steer by street-lamps and houses tonight,
In order to finish before it gets light.
Just think how the boys' and girls' faith would be shaken,
If we didn't reach 'em before they awaken!
Come Dasher! Come Dancer! Come Prancer and Vixen
Come Comet! Come Cupid! Come Donner and Blitzen!
Be quick with your suppers! Get hitched in a hurry!
You, too, will find fog a delay and a worry!"

And Santa was right. (As he usually is!)
The fog was as thick as a soda's white fizz.
Just NOT-getting-LOST needed all Santa's skill . . .
With street signs and numbers more difficult still.

He tangled
in tree-tops
    again
and again, . . .

. . . And barely
missed hitting
a tri-motored plane.

He still made good speed, with much twisting and turning,
As long as the street lamps and house lights were burning.
At each house, first noting the people who live there,
He'd quickly select the right presents to give there.
By midnight, however, the last light had fled.
(For even big people have then gone to bed!)
Because it might wake them, a match was denied him.
(Oh my, how he wished for just one star to guide him!)

Through dark streets and houses old Santa fared poorly.
He now picked the presents more slowly, less surely.
He really was worried! For what would he do,
If folks started waking before he was through?

The air was still foggy,
  the night dark and drear,
When Santa arrived
  at the home of the deer.
A ledge that he tripped-on
  while seeking the chimney
Gave Santa a spill,
  and a painfully skinned-knee.

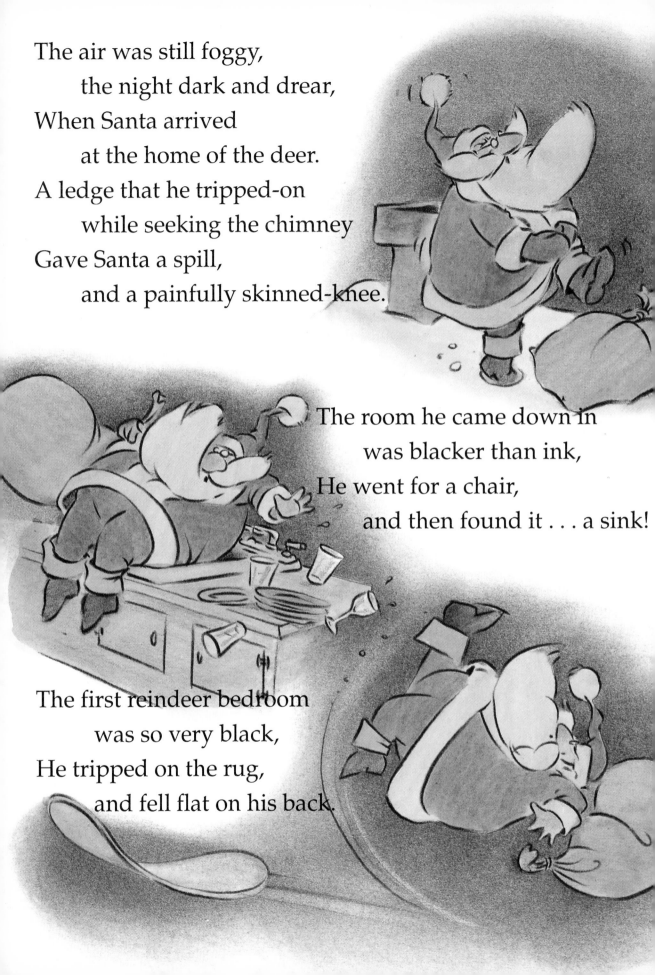

The room he came down in
  was blacker than ink,
He went for a chair,
  and then found it . . . a sink!

The first reindeer bedroom
  was so very black,
He tripped on the rug,
  and fell flat on his back.

So dark that he had to
    move close to the bed,
And squint very hard
    at the sleeping deer's head,
Before he could choose
    the right kind of a toy.
(A doll for a girl,
    or a train for a boy.)

But all this took time, and filled Santa with gloom,
While slowly he groped toward the next reindeer's room.
The door he'd just opened . . . when to his surprise,
A dim but quite definite light met his eyes.
The lamp wasn't burning; the glow came, instead,
From something that lay at the head of the bed.

And there lay . . . but wait now!
What would you suppose?
The glowing (you've guessed it)
        was . . .

. . . RUDOLPH'S RED NOSE!

So this room was easy! This one little light
Let Santa pick quickly the gifts that were right.
How happy he was, till he went out the door . . .
The rest of the house was as black as before!
So black that it made every step a dark mystery.
And then . . . came the greatest idea in all history!

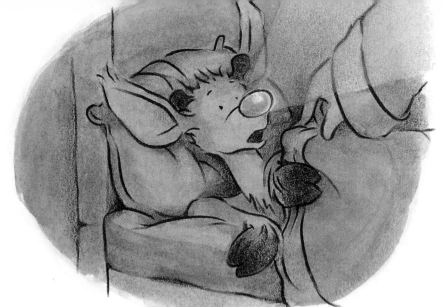

He went back to Rudolph and started to shake him
(Of course, very gently) in order to wake him.
And Rudolph could scarcely believe his own eyes!
You just can't imagine his joy and surprise
At seeing who stood there, so real and so near,
While telling the tale we've already told here:—
Poor Santa's sad tale of distress and delay . . .
The fog and the darkness, and losing the way . . .
The horrible fear that some children might waken
Before his complete Christmas trip had been taken.

"And you," he told Rudolph, "may yet save the day!
Your wonderful forehead may yet pave the way
For a wonderful triumph! It actually might!"
(Old Santa, you notice, was extra-polite
To Rudolph, regarding his "wonderful forehead."
To call it a "big, shiny nose" would sound horrid!)
"I need you," said Santa, "to help me tonight . . .
To lead all my deer on the rest of our flight."
And Rudolph broke-out into such a big grin,
It almost connected his ears and his chin!
A note for his folks he dashed-off in a hurry.
"I've gone to help Santa," he wrote. "Do not worry."
Said Santa:— "My sleigh I'll bring down to the lawn.
You'd stick in the chimney." And flash . . . he was gone.

So Rudolph pranced-out through the door, very gay,
And took his proud place at the head of the sleigh.

The rest of the night . . . well, what would you guess?
Old Santa's idea was a brilliant success.
And brilliant was almost no word for the way
That Rudolph directed the deer and the sleigh.

In spite of the fog, they flew quickly, and low,
And made such good use of the wonderful glow
From Rudolph's . . . er . . . forehead, at each intersection
That not even once did they lose their direction!
While as for the houses and streets with a sign on 'em,
They merely flew close, so that Rudolph could shine on 'em.
To tell who lived where, and just what to give whom.
They'd fly by each window and peek in the room.

BOSTON
RABBITVILLE
NEW YORK
SOUTH POLE

Old Santa knew always which children were good,
And minded their parents, and ate as they should
So Santa selected the gift that was right,
While Rudolph's . . . er . . . forehead gave just enough light.

It all went so fast, that before it was day,
The very last present was given away . . .
The very last stocking was filled to the top,
Just as the sun was preparing to pop.

This sun woke the reindeer in Rudolph's home town.
They found the short message that he'd written down . . .
They gathered outside to await his return.
And were they excited, astonished to learn
That Rudolph, the ugliest deer of them all,
(Rudolph the Red-nose . . . bashful and small . . .
The funny-faced fellow they always called names,
And practically never allowed in their games)
Was now to be envied by all far and near.
For no greater honor can come to a deer
Than riding with Santa and guiding his sleigh!
The number-one job, on the number-one day!

The sleigh, and its reindeer, soon came into view.
And Rudolph still led them, as downward they flew.
Oh boy, was he proud, as they came to a landing
Right where his handsomer playmates were standing!
These bad deer who used to do nothing but tease him
Would now have done anything . . . only to please him!

They felt even sorrier they had been bad
When Santa said:— "Rudolph, I never have had
A deer quite so brave or brilliant as you
At fighting black fog, and at guiding me through.
By YOU last night's journey was actually bossed.
Without you, I'm certain we'd all have been lost!
I hope you'll continue to keep us from grief,
On future dark trips, as COMMANDER-IN-CHIEF!"

But Rudolph just blushed, from his head to his toes,
Until his whole fur was as red as his nose!
The crowd first applauded, then started to screech:—
"Hurray for our Rudolph" and "We want a speech!"
But Rudolph was bashful, despite being a hero!
And tired! (His sleep on the trip totaled zero.)
So that's why his speech was just brief and not bright:—
"Merry Christmas to all, and to all a good night" . . .

and THAT'S why . . . .

. . . . . . whenever it's foggy and gray,
It's Rudolph the Red-nose who guides Santa's sleigh.
Be listening, this Christmas! (But don't make a peep . . .
'cause that late at night, children should be asleep!)
The very first sound that you'll hear on the roof
(Provided there's fog) will be Rudolph's small hoof.
And soon after that (if you're still as a mouse)
You may hear a "swish" as he flies 'round the house,
And gives enough light to give Santa a view
Of you and your room.
　　　　And when they're all through,
　　　　　　You may hear them call,
　　　　　　　　as they drive out of sight:—

"MERRY CHRISTMAS TO ALL,
AND TO ALL A GOOD NIGHT!"

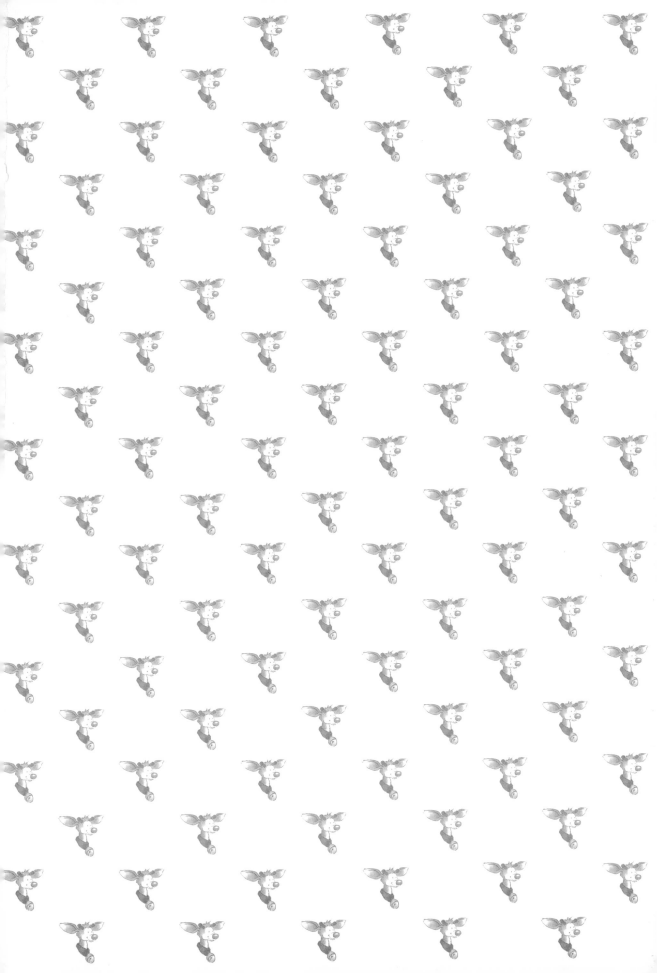

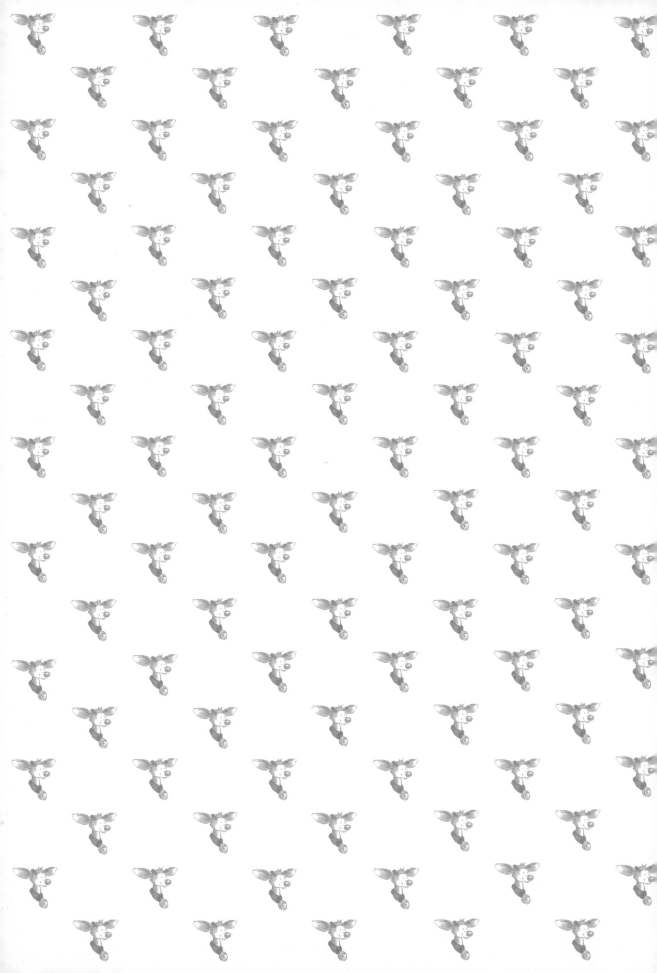